Football Mambo

Cyberworld Publishing

Cyberworld Publishing

www.CyberworldPublishing.com

First published by Cyberworld Publishing in 2014
Cover design by S Bush © 2014
Cover images: all manipulated: fish, Copyright:Alexstar, football, Copyright:robynmac, woman with gun, Copyright:Kurganov: all at Depositphotos.com
E-book ISBN: 978-1-922187-70-3
Print ISBN: 978-1-922187-71-0

Cyberworld Publishing
Jindalee St
Toronto, NSW 2283
Australia

Football Mambo

by

Peter Tonkin

Chapter One

The crane shrieked as it panned on its stand like a giant horizontal windscreen wiper, scraping the bottom of the low cloud hanging over the half-finished building across the road from my office. Adelaide was going up. I licked the chocolaty froth off the plastic lid of my take-away cappuccino and fought the urge to fortify it with a shot of brandy. Then I noticed another high-pitched noise, more rhythmic, competing with the screech of the crane. But I couldn't figure out where it was coming from. I felt something vibrating against my ribs. Then I remembered I had downloaded "Ring My Bell" as a ringtone the day before. It had cost nothing, but it had taken me hours to figure out how to do it. I took the phone out of my inside jacket pocket.

"Bruce Bilger!" I almost squealed.

A gruff voice answered, “Bruce. I’m Ken Wallis, football manager of the Centralian Galahs. We need someone discreet to handle an extremely confidential and urgent matter. Dave Ruggins suggested you might be the man for the job.”

“Well, that was nice of him. How is Dave, anyway?” Dave was one ex-colleague from my days on the police force who I could count on to say nice things about me.

“He’s good. Look, as I said, this is urgent. Can we sit down and talk about it sometime today?”

“Let me check my diary. Yes, I think I can squeeze you in . . . this morning, or this afternoon, or over lunch. I could come and see you right now if you like.”

“No, better I come and see you, say, ten o’clock. No journos hanging around your office, are there?”

“Just the usual platoon of paparazzi, fighting to be first to get a snap of my new hairstyle!”

“Let them kill each other. I’ll be right over. Your office still in Wright Street?”

“Yes, I’m still waiting for council approval to build my own skyscraper in Victoria Square.”

Ken grunted and hung up. He didn’t sound like he wanted his bell rung. He might have consented to a valve grind. I watched the crane some more while I finished my coffee and reminisced about the night I wore my paisley body shirt to the Arkaba nightclub, and that girl in the silver platforms taught me the bump. Back in the days when I actually had hair and style. Then I sat down with the morning newspaper and did some background reading.

At five to ten he banged on the door and marched in. He shook my hand the way a drunk shakes an empty beer glass to get the barman's attention and flopped down in the cantilever chair on the client's side of the desk. It sagged under his weight. Ken was a well-built man, but all the hard yards he'd put in holding up the bar were now translating into inches of excess girth.

"You follow the footy, Bruce? I mean real football—Aussie Rules."

"Yeah, of course! Always like to see the Galahs win."

"Good man! So you know what happened on Saturday then?"

"Sure, your blokes played the Cats, didn't they?" I had just learned this from the back page of the paper.

"Yeah. We lost by five points."

"Bummer. Can you still make the finals?"

"Touch and go now. We probably need to win three out of our next four games, but that's not what I'm here about."

"Just as well. Giving pep talks isn't really my strong suit."

"No, it's about something that happened during the match, something a bit odd. None of the coaching staff can figure it out. It's all here on this DVD."

I put the disc in the computer and waited for it to start up. Meanwhile, Ken set the scene for me.

"This happened during the last quarter. The Cats have

scored a behind, and Brad Spammin, our full-back, takes the kick-in, right?"

"Right."

A man with a football appeared on the screen. He kicked the ball, and one of the commentators gasped through the tinny little speakers, "I don't believe it! He's done a drop kick! I haven't seen that for thirty years!"

"Not a bad dob either. Must have travelled sixty-five metres!" added his partner.

Ken pointed a stubby finger at the computer. I hit PAUSE and he gave me a serious look that he probably wouldn't have managed at his mother's funeral.

"See what I mean?"

"Not exactly. So the guy did a drop kick. So what?"

"I'll tell you what! The coach sent the runner out to tell him to stick to drop punts, but he did another one in the last quarter. It went off the side of the boot and out of bounds without being touched, so the Cats got a free kick, and they scored a goal."

"Did that cost you the match?"

"Possibly, but nobody's blaming Brad for the loss. He played a pretty solid game, apart from those kick-ins, but this is what we can't figure out: after the match, when Bob, the coach, asked him why he'd suddenly started doing drop kicks, all Brad said was, 'The mambo made me do it.'"

"The mambo?"

"That's right, the mambo."

"As in hot Latino nights, blokes in tight dacks playing bongos and stuff?"

"Buggered if I know. I listen mostly to country and western myself."

"Me too. But what exactly do you want me to do?"

"Look, Bruce, I realise this must all sound pretty silly, but there might be more to it than meets the eye. Brad's not what you'd call a deep thinker, but he's usually reliable and calm under pressure, and this is totally out of character for him. Besides, we're concerned for his well-being. As a club, we have a duty of care towards all our players, and we take that responsibility seriously. That's why I've come to you, to ask you to investigate and find out if there's anything . . . untoward behind it, so we can put a stop to it. We'll pay you five hundred a day plus expenses. What do you say?"

I thought it over for a moment. He was right: it did sound pretty silly, but I had nothing more sensible on my plate at the moment and the rent on the office was due in three days.

"All right. I'll check it out and see what I can find out. I'll need to talk to Brad myself, and some of the other people at the club. His family too."

"Sure. I'll give you his address and home number. Talk to anyone you like—except the media. We've got to get this sorted out with a minimum of fuss so the boys can focus 110 percent on making the finals."

"Of course, I can appreciate how important that must be. But a drop kick—is it really such a big deal?"

"Look, the drop kick has no place in contemporary football. It's a total arachnidism!"

"Arak who? The Turkish wrestler?"

"Nah, you know what I mean: it's a throwback!"

"Oh, I get you. That's not allowed in AFL, is it?"

"Too bloody right it isn't!"

Chapter Two

Later that day I drove to Brad's cottage in Brompton, in the inner northwest. I opened the gate in the black-painted iron fence, navigated the stepping stones without disturbing the surrounding gravel, and rapped on the door with the shiny anchor-shaped brass doorknocker. A few seconds later footsteps scuffed across a wooden floor, a shadow obscured the fish-eye lens, and the door opened. A tall willowy blonde woman, about twenty-five, peered out at me.

"Hello?"

"Hi, my name's Bruce Bilger. Can I talk to Brad, please?"

Her face tensed up as though a hidden hand was pulling her hair.

"Ken Wallis asked me to come and, you know, debrief

him."

"Oh, OK. I suppose you'd better come in then."

I followed her down the hall and through the first door on the right. It led into the living room, where a big beefy guy sprawled on a blue denim bean bag, chewing gum mechanically. Despite his languid pose, his powerful quadriceps bulged through his track pants. No doubt he packed a hell of a kick, whatever technique he used. He didn't react at all when I came in, but when the woman said, "Brad, this is Bruce," he got to his feet, shook my hand, and said, "G'day". He was a bit bigger than me, about a hundred and ninety centimetres and a hundred kilos. He offered me a stick of the spearmint-scented gum. I took it and stuck it in my mouth, hoping that would help to forge a bond between us.

The woman walked out, almost on tiptoe, and shut the door. That simplified things. I got straight to the point and asked him why he had executed the drop kicks. The answer came as no surprise: "The mambo made me do it."

I probed him for other motives: "You reckon you can get more distance with a drop kick than a drop punt?"

"Dunno. Maybe."

I looked across the room at the brushed metal tower housing a CD collection.

"I'm really into music. Mind if I check out your CDs?"

"Go for it."

I sifted through the disks, checking the title of every track. It was mostly rock, with a bit of country, but not a drop of salsa in sight. I ploughed on, scanning the covers for anything that looked the least bit Latin. Finally, down near the bottom of the pile I found something: "Mambo Number Five." It was the second track on *Bob the Builder: The Album.* I waved the cover at him.

"Mind if I put this on?"

"Go for it."

Soon I was tapping my foot and humming along with Bob:

A little bit of timber on the roof
A little bit of making waterproof

but Brad just sat there, at one with the bean bag, immobile except for his jaw churning like a cement mixer. When the song was over, I asked him, "Did that make you feel like doing a drop kick?"

"Nah," was all he said.

A minute later he added, "Samson used to play it all the time. Gone off it now."

"Samson?"

He nodded in the direction of a metal-framed photo of a little boy in a Galahs' jumper, perched on the subwoofer box.

"He like the footy?"

"Yeah, loves it."

"Can he do a drop kick?"

"Dunno. Haven't seen him do one."

Ten minutes later I said goodbye and stepped out into the

matchbox-size front yard. The CD was under my armpit. I opened the gate and looked around like a shoplifter checking to see if security was in hot pursuit. The coast was clear. I spat out the gum. The sun crashed a pack of clouds in the west. Some of the clouds would probably need to be stretchered off. Ken had hinted that Brad wasn't exactly the sharpest tool in the shed. To me he seemed a few bayonets short of a bloodbath.

Chapter Three

On the way back to the office I was about to stop at the kebab shop, but I reminded myself that I didn't want my arteries to end up like the concrete drains beneath the road and instead picked up a couple of California rolls from Sushi Loves You.

I put the CD in the PC, sat down, and dutifully sank my teeth into the tempura prawn roll. I started to gag on the sticky rice, but I managed to wash it down with a swig of light beer. Then I shut my eyes and tried to visualise myself kicking a football. That was just as hard as acquiring a taste for sushi.

I woke up with my neck in a reef knot and "Crocodile Rock" squealing in my ears. That beer wasn't light enough, or was I turning into a lightweight? Maybe I needed to learn to like mineral water too. I might need a hypnotist's help for that.

I looked at my watch. It was about five to six. Time to call it a day. I could go home and watch TV or go to the gym and work out. Or maybe I could go and learn to mambo somewhere. It took me twenty seconds to find out that the last option was a goer. There was a beginner's class at La Bomba, just up the road in Wright Street, at a quarter past six. Fifteen bucks. The Galahs could afford it. And I might even find the answer to the great philosophical question of our time: Can you ever really mix business with pleasure?

I sort of found it. You can always combine business with pain. Mine and my instructor's. Her name was Marina and the way her hips swayed made my heart ache and my brain cells shake like the seeds in a maraca. Meanwhile, my feet went all over the place, especially on her toes. It was a lot harder than the bump. She told me I was doing fine, then muttered something under her breath about having been really bad in a previous life. Anyway, she was happy to take five, sit down, and answer a few questions.

"So, how many mambos are there, Marina?"

"How many? Hundreds, I guess. I've never tried to count them. Why?"

"Well, we've just been dancing to 'Mambo Number Nine,' right, and there's a 'Mambo Number Eight' too, isn't there? So, do they fit into some list or catalogue or something?"

"Not that I know." She bent her lips into a smile, while bewilderment pushed her eyelids back.

"And some of them have lyrics—mostly in Spanish as far

as I can tell."

"Yes, but they're not tremendously deep, you know, it's mostly stuff like, '*Que rico el mambo!*' or '*Si si si, quiero mambo!*' It's a bit like the Beatles singing, 'Yeah yeah yeah!'"

"Right, but didn't they say that some of the Beatles' songs had hidden messages in them, like if you played them backwards you would hear, 'Paul is dead!' or something?"

She leaned back a fraction, as if afraid that whatever I had might be contagious.

"I know nothing about that. Excuse me, I have to go to the bathroom."

I excused her. A minute later I limped out to the car park myself. I felt like I'd strained a groin muscle. I should have done a warm-up before I started my pathetic attempt to mambo. Still, I was keen to continue with my research, so I drove a few blocks north to Rundle Street and found Big Star Records open.

There was a Goth behind the counter, smiling dreamily to some throbbing hypnotic grunge. Her left earring was made from one of those little syringe attachments you screw onto a bike pump to inflate a football. I had to shout to get her attention.

"Hello! Got any mambo records?"

She looked at me blankly.

"You know: salsa, Latin music. Got a world music section?"

"Oh yeah, over there." She pointed in the general direction of Cuba.

I found *Mondo Mambo* and *Voodoo Suite* by Perez Prado and took them to the counter. The two of them together only set me back nineteen ninety-five. The Goth still looked like she was lost in space, but she managed to give me five cents change.

On the way back to the office I bought some corn chips. Nacho cheese flavour sounded like it ought to create the right ambience. I put *Mondo Mambo* on, sat down, and opened the packet. Some of it sounded vaguely familiar, but Señor Prado's version of "Mambo Number Five" was radically different from Bob's, and "Virgen de la Macarena" was nothing like that other "Macarena" song that you used to hear everywhere a few years ago. And I was none the wiser at the end of it. A bit of googling told me that the increased pace of the game and changes to boot design had brought about the demise of the drop kick in AFL football. A victim of progress.

I went back to my maisonette in Mile End, kicked back in the chocolate leather recliner, closed my eyes, and listened to "Voodoo Suite." It was savage, primeval music. I could imagine Brad committing mass murder to it, but not doing a drop kick, drop punt or mongrel punt. I opened my eyes again. The ceiling needed painting. I brushed the scum of nacho and wasabi off my teeth and went to bed.

I woke up in the middle of a dream where I was trying to pump up a football with a Tabasco sauce bottle. The ball turned into a fish that had sequins on it instead of scales. Then it giggled and said, "Spice me up Shiny!" It was a voice I recognised. But whose? Owen somebody. He used to be in Forensics, but he was supposed to have quit and set up his own lab. High-tech stuff. Maybe I should take these mambo records to him and have him analyse them. If there were subliminal messages somewhere telling Brad to do a drop kick, that guy would be sure to find them.

I got up and rummaged through the chocolate box with all the business cards in it until I found his. Owen Davies. Forensonics. Sound engineering and analysis. Digital and analog. Address in Rundle Street Kent Town and other contact details. Number one smartarse.

It was just after four thirty. I toyed with the idea of ringing him then and waking him up, but thought better of it and went back to bed. I could feel fish slithering around in my guts. I could have sworn they were dead when I ate them. I got up again and drank a beer to settle my stomach. Eventually, I fell asleep again.

I woke up at about seven and lurched out of bed with all the agility of a beached whale. I hobbled to the bathroom. After a few minutes under a hot shower, I could move a bit more freely. I strode to the kitchen like a man. I ate toast. I drank coffee. I called Owen Davies and told him what I needed done. He confirmed that it was the sort of thing he could do. He said he would be free at half past eleven. Then I rang Barbara Trevellyan, the manager of the Paradise Billabong, and arranged to meet her there an hour later. People who work in bars pick up a lot of useful information with the empty beer glasses.

Rundle Street Kent Town is a mixed residential and

commercial extension of Adelaide's main shopping strip on the other side of the East Parklands. Number fifteen was a bluestone cottage. A new silver Audi was parked out the front.

Owen's 'lab' was in the front room. It didn't look or smell like a lab: no test tubes, no chemical odours. I stood in the corner and looked at all the brushed black metal boxes and tried to figure out what they were all for.

"So how's business? Can't be too bad, judging by the look of things."

He sat behind his shiny futuristic desk and patted his ergonomic keyboard. He had a goatee now. It helped to camouflage his pasty face, but it did nothing to hide the self-satisfied smirk.

"Yeah, it's going well. Of course it's not just the forensics, I'm doing some networking stuff as well, and several other projects will come on stream soon. What about yourself?"

"Oh, can't complain. Keeping busy enough." Why didn't I just hold up a sign saying LOSER?

He said he could probably give me a preliminary assessment within twenty-four hours, so I left him to it. Ten minutes in the same room as him was enough to send my blood pressure higher than any umpire could bounce the ball.

Chapter Four

I drove about ten kilometres up the Lower North-East Road to Paradise Stadium, the Galahs' home ground. I parked in the shadow of the concrete coliseum and found the Paradise Billabong. I trekked across a vast expanse of burgundy carpet, inhaling the aroma of stale beer with every step, to the semicircular bar. It had a sort of palisade veneer on it. Maybe that was supposed to make the patrons feel like they were marooned on a tropical island and dying of thirst. It was working a treat for me.

Barbara was standing behind the bar. She was a forty-something, no-nonsense woman with short brown hair and a much slicker business card than mine. But then just about everyone had one of those. I really needed to do something about that. Maybe when my inheritance came through.

Still, she studied my card respectfully enough and then laid it on the bar, a safe distance from the beer tray.

"A private detective, eh? Do you drink on the job?"

I clenched my fists and my teeth, fought the temptation with every sinew in my body, and shook my head.

"Not unless I really need to, like if I'm trying to get someone to talk. I bet you could drink me under the table."

"Not these days, love. I have to watch my weight and look after my liver. Can I get you a ginger ale or something?"

"Yeah, that'd be good, thanks."

She poured two and put one on the bar in front of me.

"There you go. Now, how can I help?"

"You know why I'm here?"

"Sort of. It's got something to do with Brad, hasn't it?"

"Yeah. What I'm thinking is, maybe someone's got to him, someone obsessed with bringing back the drop kick, and it's possible that person is a member of the club. So I'm wondering if you can recall ever hearing any of your patrons getting nostalgic about the drop kick and agitating for its return, or anything along those lines."

She laughed and said, "Listen love, if I had a dollar for every time I've heard some piss-head yabbering on about bringing back the drop kick and the stab pass, I could forget about the water restrictions and hose down the car park with Veuve Cliquot."

She put down the brandy balloon she was polishing and screwed up her face, as though her teeth were connected to her memory by strings and rubber bands. Then something went *twang* behind her eyes and they widened.

"Actually, though, now that you mention it, there were these two blokes who used to drink here, and they were *deadly* serious about it. They'd go on and on about it for hours. We used to call them 'The Odd Couple'. But I haven't seen them round here for a while."

"Don't remember their names, either of them, do you?"

"Wait a minute, it'll come to me. The older gent with the beard and the beer belly, he was an ex-footballer, used to have a fishing show too. Wally Grunt!"

The name meant nothing to me, but I nodded and wrote it down.

"And why did you call them 'The Odd Couple'?"

"Because the other bloke was the exact opposite. He was some kind of scientist, a total nerd, and he'd rave on about the tragedy of the drop kick and stuff."

"Tragedy? As in its untimely demise?"

"I don't know. 'Low tragedy,' he called it."

"You mean low *trajectory*? Like in ballistics?"

"Yeah, maybe that was it. It was real technical stuff anyway. Went way over my head and everyone else's, but Wally would just lap it up and thump the table and shout, 'Yes, yes!' I felt a bit sorry for the nerdy guy. He looked a real mess, but all the blokes thought he was a scream. Can't remember his name for the life of me, though."

"And do you remember ever seeing Brad Spammin drinking with them?"

"No, I never saw him or any of the players with those two."

"That's OK. You've been a big help, Barbara. By the way, do you know if these blokes were members?"

"Well, at least one of them must've been, because I never saw anyone else sign them in. Why don't you have a word with Simon, the membership manager? He might be able to tell you more. I'll ring and see if he's around if you like."

Simon was around. Barbara showed me up to his office herself. On the way she filled me in on his illustrious playing career, cut short by a persistent knee injury. I could relate to that. I still hadn't recovered from my abortive attempt to mambo. I was glad we took the lift and not the stairs.

Simon was there, waiting for us, when the lift doors opened. He was in his mid-thirties, shaven-headed, about a hundred and eighty-five centimetres tall. He grinned, said, "G'day" and pumped my hand, then nodded to Barbara and grunted, "Thanks Babs". You could hardly spot it in the tailored charcoal suit, but he limped the tiniest bit as he showed me into his office.

It offered him a panoramic view of the oval if he swivelled away from his desk. That looked like a dangerous distraction for an ex-player. There were wall-to-wall filing cabinets on one side, and above them a big framed photograph of the Centralian Galahs premiership team. After studying it for a few seconds I could make him out as the lean, hard-bodied man crouching in the middle row. I didn't need to explain much to him. The club was closing ranks behind Brad Spammin with an esprit de corps that made the Three Musketeers look like a circus of backstabbers.

Simon's fingers flew over the keys the way he used to fly over the pack, if Barbara was to be believed.

"Wally Grunt, Wally Grunt," he muttered. "Got him! Membership lapsed at the end of the 2004 season. Twenty-fourth October to be precise."

"I see. Did you know him personally?"

"Yeah no, everyone did. He was a legend—one of the old-time hard men. I can remember watching him play when I was a kid. Hard as nails, but he had real skill as well. He'd shirt-front a bloke, grab the ball, and then wheel onto his left boot and just drill a sixty-metre drop kick bang onto the full-forward's chest. He was a real champion."

"Got an address or a phone number?"

"Yeah no, we don't normally give them out, but in this case I guess it's OK. He might have moved anyway." He scribbled the number on a sticky note and passed it across the desk.

"Of course, it stays confidential. When the case is closed I'll destroy the details."

"Thanks, we'd all appreciate that."

"Barbara said he used to drink with another bloke who was a bit of an egghead. Any idea who that might've been?"

He stopped grinning. "What do you mean, 'egghead'?"

"A boffin. Some kind of scientist."

"Oh. Don't remember anyone like that."

"He might have been a member too."

"No kidding! Do you know how many members this club has, Bruce?"

"No idea."

"About fifty thousand. I've probably met about ten thousand of them in person, but I can't remember them all."

"Fair enough."

We sat there and thought our separate thoughts for a minute. The two white goalposts in the background looked like a pair of antennae sprouting from the shiny dome of his head. A football sailed between them and disappeared. Then I had an idea that came about as close to inspiration as a mug like me ever gets.

"Could you do a search on your computer for people whose membership lapsed within, say, three months of Wally's, and see if that gets us anywhere?"

"I wouldn't have a clue how to do that. I'm not exactly a wizard when it comes to computers. But I could get the IT geek here and see if he can do it."

He rang someone called Steve. Steve didn't take long to appear. He was a gawky youth with reddish hair who looked like he should have been in a school blazer instead of a suit. He seemed to know his IT onions though. It only took him about three minutes to "query the database" and generate a report with seventy-two names and contact details.

Back in the bar, Barbara ran her eye over the printout. About two-thirds of the way down she stopped. She muttered to herself and closed her eyes. After a second she opened them wide, smiled, and tapped the paper with a cerise nail.

"Lucas Stokes! That's gotta be him!"

Chapter Five

I drove back to the office, stopping on the way to get some Vietnamese prawn rolls, and started searching for the odd couple.

Nobody answered the phone number Simon had given me, but it only took a minute of searching the net to find an old photo of Wally Grunt in his football kit, arms crossed and eyeballing the camera like a blue heeler staring down a wayward sheep. Then I found the website of *Modern Angler*, a magazine he now edited.

On the "Contact us" page there was a phone number. I rang it. A young woman answered. I asked for Wally. She put him on. He said he was flat out trying to make the deadline for the next month's issue, but he would be happy to talk to me after that. We settled on one p.m. the next day, in his office. He didn't ask me what I wanted, even after I told him I was a private detective.

There was an online readers' poll on the website. The sixty-four-dollar question was: "Is fishing better than sex?"

There were four possible answers:

1. Yes
2. No
3. No, but it's a lot safer
4. Fishing IS the new sex!

I clicked on Number 2. That brought up a graph showing that I was a member of a tiny minority. Possibly an even smaller and more marginal group than the 'bring back the drop kick' mob.

Then I started looking for Lucas. I rang the landline number on Steve's list. A woman answered.

"Hello."

"Hello, could I speak to Lucas Stokes please?"

"With regard to what?"

"Well, it's in relation to football—and physics."

"Really?" She sounded half-curious, half-amused. Then there was a long silence. "Are you a colleague of his?"

I paused for a moment too. Maybe I could try to bluff my way through this one, but my inner bookie told me the odds weren't good. Her accent wasn't exactly posh, but it was cultivated. It came out of a throat that could tell burgundy from brake fluid. So I decided to level with her.

"No, I'm a private detective."

"You're kidding!" Sometimes it's an uphill struggle to stay

on the level.

"No, fair dinkum. I've got a licence and everything."

"I see! So what exactly are you investigating, and what's it got to do with football and physics?"

"Well, it's kind of complicated. Excuse me, but does Mr Stokes live there?"

"No. Not these days."

"Ah. So, if you don't mind me asking, are you his ex-partner?"

"No and yes."

"Pardon?"

"No, I don't mind, and yes, I am."

"I see. And would you be able to apprise me of his current whereabouts?"

"No, I'm afraid I have no idea where he is."

"I see. Still, I'd appreciate it if you could spare a few minutes. You might be able to point me in the right direction."

"By all means. How about tomorrow morning, about ten thirty?"

"Fine with me. Where?"

"I'll be at home. I suppose you know the address?"

"If you haven't moved in the last three years."

"I'm afraid I've gone nowhere in the last three years. Can I ask you a question, Mr.—what did you say your name was?"

"Bilger, Bruce Bilger."

"My name's Julie, Bruce. But I suppose you knew that

already."

"No I didn't. I don't know anything about you."

"Well, that's mildly reassuring. By the way, Bruce, when you show up here tomorrow, will you be packing?"

"You mean, carrying a firearm? No, I don't see any need for that. I've got no reason to regard you as dangerous."

She sighed. "Perhaps that's my problem."

"I see." I didn't really, and I didn't want to. "So, I'll see you tomorrow at ten thirty."

"Sure. Bye."

I figured I had done enough work for one day. I went to the pub on the corner, had a counter meal and a drop of the house red, then went home and watched a DVD of *Saturday Night Fever* and went to bed.

Chapter Six

The next morning I went to the office before going to see Julie. I was checking the mail when there was a buzz at the door.

"Come in! It's open!" I shouted.

The door swung open a few inches, and Brad's wife peered around it and scrutinised the office. Then she stepped inside and closed the door behind her. When she took off her sunglasses I could see the shadows of sleepless nights under her eyes. I offered her the chair and a glass of the brandy that I kept in the first-aid kit in case of emergency. She hesitated a moment and then nodded. I poured myself a small one by way of providing moral support.

"I'm sorry to just barge in like this, without an appointment or anything, Mr. Bilger."

"That's all right. Call me Bruce. Sorry, what's your name again?"

"Tamara. I picked up your business card when I was vacuuming. I don't know if I should be here, but I'm so worried about Brad, and I don't know who to talk to about it."

"What exactly are you worried about? This drop kick business?"

"It's not just that. I can't really put my finger on it, but he's been acting so strange lately."

"In what way?"

"Oh I don't know, little things, like he talks in his sleep, which he never used to do. Not that I noticed anyway."

"I see. And can you understand what he says when he does that?"

"Not much, just this one phrase: 'thirty-nine degrees', over and over."

"Thirty-nine degrees? Any idea what that means?"

"No, I asked him about it once when he woke up, but he just grunted and said he couldn't remember. I mean, he's never been what you'd call a big talker, but lately I can hardly get a word out of him—when he's awake. He's like a total stranger."

I refilled her glass and took a sip out of mine. Just to be sociable.

"Can you remember exactly when this change came about?"

"Hard to say, but I remember thinking he was awfully

moody when he came back from a fishing trip a couple of weeks ago."

"Any idea where he went?"

"Not really. Up the coast somewhere, I think."

"Uh-huh. And when he came back, did anything in his demeanour or behaviour strike you as odd?"

"Well for starters, he didn't bring back any fish, just some poor man's asparagus."

"What poor man?"

"No, that's just what they call it. It's a vegetable. It's supposed to be good for your digestion. Anyway, I steamed it and we had it with some fish fingers. Wasn't bad actually. Still, it made me wonder how much fishing he'd really been doing."

"And who did he go fishing, or asparagus-hunting, with?"

"Kane, I suppose. He usually goes fishing with him."

"Who's Kane?"

"Kane Jordan. He plays half-back flank, and he's Brad's best mate at the club. People say they have this telepathic understanding on the football field. I wish I did. Not on the football field, of course. But talking to Brad doesn't seem to get me anywhere."

"Yeah, well, communication, it's a tricky thing, isn't it? Especially for men. Most blokes are lousy communicators, present company included."

"You married, Bruce?"

"Well, legally speaking I still am, but . . ."

"Separated?"

"Yeah. My wife left about three years ago."

"What happened? You cheat on her—what's her name?"

"Dianne. No, actually, it was her who . . ."

"Found another bloke?"

"No, she went a bit, you know, hotel-motel, and ran off with a forensic cosmetician, another policewoman. We were both in the police force back then."

"Someone from work? That must have been tough."

"Yeah, it was a bit. Policemen have a pretty crude sense of humour."

"I can just imagine! I bet they took the piss out of you big time!"

"Yeah, you might say that. Still, worse things happen at sea."

"And she dumped you for another woman! You poor thing! Geez, I don't know what I'd do if I found out that Brad was rooting another bloke. Another woman, I could sort of cope with that, but a man!"

She slammed her glass down on the desk. I almost jumped.

"You don't think that could be it, do you?"

"What, that Brad's turned gay on you? Nah, I don't think that's it."

"How do you know?"

"Well I don't, but I don't see any reason to think so."

"Listen, Bruce, will you promise me something?"

"Yeah, sure, if I find out that he has gone queer and he's cheating on you with Kane or any other bloke, I'll let you know straight away."

I had my fingers crossed behind my back. She wasn't my client anyway.

"Thanks, Bruce, I'd really appreciate that." She got up and left, a little unsteadily.

Thirty-nine degrees. Was that too hot to mambo, or just hot enough?

Chapter Seven

It was a quarter past ten. I had only had half a nip of brandy, so I figured I should be OK to drive. In post-rush-hour traffic it only took me about ten minutes to get to Julie's house in a leafy street in Unley. It was a charming old bluestone cottage with slate stepping stones snaking through the low-maintenance native ground cover in the front yard. There was a black wrought-iron gorgon's head on the door. I looked away as I knocked. Clogs clacked on wooden floorboards. The door swung open.

She looked about fifty, one sixty-eight centimetres tall, reddish-brown hair that might have been largely henna, not much makeup. Blue-grey eyes flicked up and down, sizing me up. She smiled.

"Hello. Bruce, I presume?"

"Yeah. Hi, Julie, thanks for seeing me at such short notice."

"Don't mention it. Come in."

I followed her up the hall and into the living room. We sat down on a red corduroy sofa that was getting a bit threadbare. There was a crack in the wall above the open fireplace. There might have been more cracks hiding behind the bookshelves covering two walls, or the abstract art. No TV. A record player and lots of vinyl. Maybe she collected books and records. Some people spend all their money on that kind of stuff.

"Coffee? Tea? Something harder?"

"Coffee would be good, thanks. It's a bit early for the hard stuff."

"Times have changed. It was never too early for Marlowe."

"Who's Marlowe?"

"Never mind. Milk, sugar, cyanide?"

"Just milk, thanks."

I breathed into my hand while she was out of the room. She wouldn't need to be a police dog to smell brandy. I fumbled for a mint and slipped it in my mouth just before she came back. She put an exquisitely crafted turquoise and cobalt mug on the chunky wooden coffee table. The mug looked like the most expensive thing in the room. I felt a bit apprehensive about picking it up. Next to it was a little book: *A Jerk at One End. Confessions of a Mediocre Fisherman.* Somehow I couldn't picture her reading that.

She leaned back into the corner of the sofa and turned forty-five degrees to face me. "So, what's this all about?"

I gave her a brief outline, omitting Brad's name. She listened intently and nodded.

"And you think Lucas might be involved in this somehow?"

"I don't know. I don't have much to go on at the moment. All I know is he and an ex-footballer called Wally Grunt used to be members of the Centralian Galahs Football Club and drink in the club bar, the Paradise Billabong, and talk about the drop kick a lot. Then their memberships lapsed and they haven't been seen there since then. I'm trying to find out whether they are still in contact and whether either or both of them are implicated in this . . . situation."

"I see. And you know Lucas wrote his doctoral thesis on the physics of the drop kick?"

I didn't, but she didn't need to know that. "Yes, actually, I was wondering if I could have a look at it."

"I don't know if there's still a copy of it around here anywhere. Some of Luke's papers are still stashed away in boxes in the garage, but I haven't set foot in there for ages. It would probably be quicker and easier to search for it in the Barr-Smith Library. And there'd be fewer red-backs around."

"The what library?"

"The Barr-Smith—the university library. They keep copies of all doctoral theses by Adelaide University students."

"I see. Have you read it?"

"Me? Hell no! I'm an anthropologist, not a physicist. I wouldn't understand a word of it, or an equation. He did try to explain it to me in very simple terms when we started going out. I vaguely recall something about its having superior directional stability due to the extra backspin. And there was a whole chapter devoted to the optimal angle."

"The optimal angle?"

"Yes, for the kick to be most effective, it should hit the ground at a certain angle to the horizontal."

"Thirty-nine degrees?"

"Yes, I think that might have been it."

"And did he follow the football? Was he a fan?"

"Yes, he was, in a way. So was I, in a way."

"Really? I never would have guessed."

"Sure, we were the backbone of the Sturt Cheer Squad! No, seriously, that's how we met. I was doing my thesis on the football club as neo-tribal construct, using Sturt Football Club as a case study. My supervisor thought they were a bit too middle class and recommended that I study Port Adelaide instead, but I wanted to demonstrate that the tribal identity was not circumscribed by Marxian class boundaries. And besides, Unley Oval was just up the road. Still is. And that's where I ran into Lucas, keenly observing the players practising their drop kicks. Sturt were the masters of the art back then."

"Weren't they just? And how long did Lucas spend

studying the drop kick?"

"The thesis took him three or four years. He spent a lot of time in the lab as well, doing computer modelling, which seemed terribly high-tech at the time, but was really primitive by today's standards."

"I bet. And how did he go—did he pass?"

"Yes, you might say that. His thesis was very well received, and he obtained a fellowship to do post-doctoral research as well as doing some teaching."

"And did he seem to be obsessed with it; did he keep talking about it?"

"Not really. I mean, we'd both *done* football. I'd finished my thesis too. We got married soon afterwards, and we both moved on to other things. He watched it a bit on TV, but he hardly ever went to matches."

"And then—sorry if I'm prying into your private life, but—what happened between you and him? I mean, did you just drift apart, the way people do, or was there . . . ?"

"Someone else? Well might you ask! In a way there was, actually. You see, he took up fishing, which I just couldn't understand. I couldn't see the appeal of it at all. He'd just disappear for the whole night, and then say he'd been at Glenelg Jetty, or he'd go away for the whole weekend, to Goolwa or somewhere, and I began to suspect it was just an alibi, that he was seeing someone else, although in retrospect that seems rather unlikely; after all, he's not exactly Casanova. I toyed with the idea of hiring a private detective, but then I put on my trench coat and gumshoes and followed him myself instead, only to find that he really was going fishing with these boring old wallies."

"And was Wally Grunt one of these . . . . wallies?"

"I've no idea what their names were. One time I sat in the car and watched them through binoculars all night. They just sat on folding chairs on Brighton Jetty, in their flannel shirts and those knitted hats like tea cosies, talking about god-knows-what. Unfortunately, I didn't have a parabolic microphone or anything to pick up what they were talking about—come to think of it maybe that wasn't so unfortunate—but eventually I fell asleep, and I actually got back after him, and then we had this screaming row. I walked in and he was trying to cook this squid or something for breakfast, it was the only thing he'd caught, and I must have looked an absolute fright, I suppose. He asked me where I'd been and started insinuating that I was having an affair! He didn't have the guts to accuse me straight out, and in the end I sort of gave him an ultimatum: me or the fish. The fish won."

"Really? And what happened then? He moved out?"

"Yes. I came back from work one day and he'd gone. Taken the car and his clothes, not much else. No forwarding address."

"And when was this?"

"Two years ago today."

There was a long silence, such as a couple of anglers might share on a starlit jetty. Scrounging for a way to restart the conversation, I glanced down at the book.

"You reading this?"

"Yes." She laughed. "I decided to make a serious effort to understand the fascination of fishing. After all, if Robert Hughes could be so passionate about it, then why shouldn't Lucas?"

"Fair enough." I went for a long shot: "You don't subscribe to *Modern Angler* by any chance, do you?"

"I don't subscribe to modern anything. I'm a postmodernist."

"Forensic?"

"Well, I have dabbled in forensic discourse analysis, now that you mention it."

"Is that something to do with conversations with the dead?"

"Hmm, I've certainly had my fair share of conversations with the brain dead."

Was she having a go at me, or was I getting a bit out of my depth? I felt like a five-year-old kid hanging onto a leaking inner tube and drifting out with the tide, beyond the continental shelf, and into the shark-infested waters of the Timor Sea.

"And so, you don't have any contact with Lucas these days?"

"No, I never see him on campus, I don't know what he's doing or where he lives or what he lives on. I've tried to call him on his mobile, just to ask if he's all right, but it just goes straight to his voicemail and he never calls back. Lately I've been trying to dream up some fish-oriented message that might get through to him, but inspiration doesn't always come when you most need it."

"Yeah, well, they say fishing's a waiting game."

"Lucas once tried to tell me it was about occupying the same quantum space as the fish."

"Is that right? Was he on drugs, do you think?"

"No, but he probably should have been. Once he got started about fishing and string theory and all the rest of it, he'd get so excited he needed something to calm him down, although he claimed it relaxed him. It would certainly calm me down. Calm me into a coma."

I had to bite my tongue to stop myself saying, "I bet you'd look good in a coma!" When notions that stupid start springing to mind I know it's time to make myself scarce, so I stood up and said, "Well, I won't take up any more of your time. Thanks for the coffee. By the way, would you have a photo of Lucas I could borrow?"

She went out and came back a minute later with a photo of a man, about forty, with gold-rimmed glasses and a faraway look. It looked a few years old. I tried to picture him with less hair and an even more distant gaze. Then I gave her the usual spiel: If you should happen to hear from him or remember anything relevant, don't hesitate to contact me, etc. Then I gave her my card. She didn't turn her nose up at it like it was a three-day-old fish. At least she didn't seem to think I was cheap then, even if she thought I was a jerk. That was something.

Chapter Eight

I stopped at a café on Unley Road and had a grilled cheese sandwich and a tomato juice. Then I went to see Wally. *Modern Angler*'s nerve centre was an office on the third floor of a newish building on Greenhill Road, just south of the CBD. One of the glass doors was open. I tapped on it and walked into a big room, broken up by free-standing orange partitions adorned with fishing calendars and posters. Half-hidden behind one of the partitions was a huge, irregularly shaped desk made of driftwood, with a wide-screen computer monitor on it. I took another stride and saw a hairy man, pushing sixty, seated behind it. Apart from his belly spilling onto the desk, he didn't look too different from his picture on the web.

"Wally? I'm Bruce Bilger."

"G'day Bruce! Come in and pull up a pew!" he shouted. He didn't get up or even look up. He just kept typing and chewing on one end of his greying walrus moustache.

He did nod towards the corner and bark, "Help yourself to coffee! There should be a bit left." I wandered over, found an off-white china cup and half-filled it with what looked and smelled like slightly diluted tar from a filter apparatus on top of a filing cabinet. It had probably been stewing all night. I couldn't see any milk or sugar. I sipped the bitter black liquid and looked out at the gum trees and goalposts in the parklands across the road. Then I turned around to see Wally muttering to himself as his red-rimmed eyes swivelled from side to side, as though following a fly buzzing across the screen. He seemed to have forgotten that I was there.

"Sorry if I'm disturbing you, Wally. I thought your deadline would have passed by now."

"That was for the print edition. Now I'm working on the on-line version, analysing the results of the readers' poll."

"Oh yeah, I saw that. Interesting."

He guffawed and winked at me. "Mate, whatever you're flogging, hook it up to sex somehow, any old how, and you're halfway there, right? Sex sells. Sex gets people talking."

"Sure, can't argue with that. So, uh, how long have you been putting this magazine out, Wally?"

He paused for a moment, looked up, and grinned, revealing two rows of discoloured teeth that would probably bite as hard as a white pointer if the right bait was dangled in front of them.

"Next month she'll be five years old!"

"That's quite an achievement. Must have taken a lot of work, keeping it going all this time."

"Tell me about it, mate! It was a real tough slog getting it off the ground—I never left the office hardly for the first year or so. That wasn't here, we used to operate out of my back shed!"

"No bull! You've come a long way then. This is quite an impressive setup."

"Yeah, nice isn't it? But the main thing is we've got some real bright kids with fresh ideas and skills on board, and now we're reaching a whole new demographic. Lots of young people go fishing, you know, not just old farts like me—people from all different backgrounds, including women. We're all multicultural these days. We've even got some articles in Mandarin and Vietnamese on the web version!"

"Really? By the way, speaking of technical people, do you know a bloke called Lucas Stokes?"

The grin retreated behind his moustache, and just for a moment he looked at me like I was a stingray skulking at the bottom of a tidal pool. Then his face went blank.

"Don't think so. Should I? Is he a web designer or something?"

"No, he's a physicist actually. I heard you used to sink a few with him down at the Paradise Billabong."

"No kidding? Well, if you looked real hard, you might find a dozen blokes in this town I haven't blown froth at in that place! Are you looking for this bloke?"

"Yeah, his missus asked me to track him down. He did a runner on her."

"Really? Why? Bit of a dragon, is she?"

"Didn't strike me that way. But you never can tell, can you?"

"No, you sure can't. Fish are a lot easier to figure out."

"I bet. Anyway, thanks for your time, Wally."

"No problem, but I'm damned if I know why anyone told you I could help you find this bloke. What did you say his name was?"

"Lucas Stokes."

"Lucas Stokes, Lucas Stokes. No, still doesn't ring any bells."

"Fair enough. It's just I heard you and he shared a passion for the drop kick."

"Passion for the drop kick? That sounds a bit kinky."

"Well, they say you used to talk quite a lot about how it should be brought back into the game."

"Really? Well, it pains me deeply to admit it, Bruce, but that's probably not the stupidest thing I ever said when I was pissed. That's why I don't hang around the Paradise Billabong, or any other pub, bar, inn or tavern, any more. I've got better things to do, and I can do them better when I'm sober."

“Would that include doing any actual fishing? It looks like the magazine takes up most of your time.”

“Oh, I still get out on the water on weekends and bring home something for dinner, don’t you worry! Anyway, have an advance copy, on the house! It won’t hit the news stands for a couple of days yet.”

He tossed it to me across the desk. I hope I faked gratitude better than he faked being on the wagon.

Chapter Nine

I took a detour on the way back to the office. Instead of going west up Greenhill Road, I headed east towards the Adelaide Hills for about half a kilometre, and then I turned left into a gravelled area on the edge of the South Parklands. I parked the car and got out, nodding to a few people walking their dogs as I walked towards the tents scattered among the gum trees. A handful of people had been living there since the housing crisis got serious. If Lucas had a car, he could hang out there for a long time without spending much money. I wandered around and chatted to half a dozen of the inhabitants, some young, some old, all men with despair in their eyes. I didn't find Lucas, but one of the tent dwellers recognised him from the photo. He told me that he'd left that morning, promising to return in a couple of days with fish for everyone.

"So he's still got a car then?"

"Yeah, that's his crate over there. They went in the other bloke's car."

"What other bloke?"

"Some wanker who walks his dog over there at the racetrack." He pointed north.

"Why do you reckon he's a wanker?"

"What kind of bloke drives a purple Saab and has a bull terrier called Sharon?"

"One of them, I suppose. Any idea who he is and what his connection to Lucas is?"

"Nope. He's never mentioned the dude, and we don't ask each other too many questions here."

"Fair enough, but if there's anything you've noticed, even any wild guesses, I'd appreciate it. Nobody needs to know it came from you." I gave him my best "you can trust me" look and a twenty-dollar note. He stuffed the note in the pocket of his jeans and drew circles in the gravel with his foot for a minute. Then he spoke.

"Well, I got no idea who the wanker is, but a couple of weeks ago I went to the bottle shop at the Arkaba to buy some grog, and I bumped into Lucas coming out of the betting shop in there. He had a big smile on his face, but he seemed really embarrassed when he saw me. I just nodded and acted like nothing was up. Then just as I was coming out, I saw the Saab pull up on the other side of the road and Lucas jump in. Didn't see him for a few days after that."

"Hmmm, interesting. Thanks for that. Of course we never had this conversation, but I'd be grateful if you could call me if Lucas turns up again." I gave him my card and another twenty.

I went back to the office and tried to figure out my next move. Should I concentrate on finding Lucas, or approach Kane, or follow Wally? And who could the man with the bull terrier be?

"Ring My Bell" interrupted my ruminations again. It was Owen. He had finished his analysis and suggested I come and collect it and the CDs. For some reason he didn't want to tell me about it over the phone. I figured Kane could wait, so I went straight over.

He received me with exaggerated warmth, even offering me a cappuccino from the shiny new red-and-black machine in his office. It was a lot better than Wally's coffee. I sat on the chair opposite his desk and stirred the chocolate powder into the froth while I waited for him to get to the point. He didn't, so I prompted him.

"So what have we got?"

"Nothing. I've analysed every track on the CD. Whether played backwards or forwards, fast or slow, none of them contain any subliminal or coded messages. It's just music—if you call that music," he sneered. Contempt came easily to him.

"Why couldn't you tell me this over the phone?"

He oscillated in his swivel chair and pressed the fingertips of both hands together. "Well, Bruce, there's something else that I—we—need to clarify. Nothing to do with music."

"And what would that be?"

"Well, it's something more to do with fishing, actually."

Now I knew where he was coming from. He was talking about an afternoon in St Vincent's Gulf about five years before. Five men in a boat. A friendly fishing trip, just a few mates, a couple of slabs and any fish that were cooperative enough to bite. It was real matey for an hour or so. But after the fourth beer I began to sense an evil undertow beneath the froth. Something had been set up, and something or someone was going to go down. Was it me? If not, what was I there for? How well did I know these blokes anyway?

Well, Chris was in the CIB with me, so I knew him fairly well, or thought I did. Thommo and Craigo were in the Drug Squad, and Daz was somehow connected with them, as an informant or something. It didn't seem like a good idea to ask exactly what he was or did. It didn't seem like a good idea to argue when the others started heaving him off the boat either. I just looked the other way and cracked another tube.

Thommo winked as he wiped his hands on his combat pants and said, "Don't worry mate! Nobody saw him get on the boat!"

We did come back with some fish. I took one home for tea. Dianne was a bit surprised, but she fried it in butter and it tasted great with a bit of lemon juice. I don't know that I adequately conveyed my appreciation of her culinary efforts, but then I was a bit preoccupied.

And with good reason. It transpired that Daz had been summoned as a witness at a coronial inquest, and his failure to appear had serious repercussions. Superintendent Watson called us in one by one and grilled us about the outing. Someone, it seemed, had seen Daz get on the boat. I told him there had been an accident, but I hadn't seen it because I was taking a leak off the starboard side while Daz fell over the port. The others told me they had all come up with similarly convincing alibis. We all started looking at each other sideways, wondering if one of us had blabbed. I started to sense the cloud of suspicion darkening over me.

I stayed on the force for another year or two, but soon realised my career was going nowhere. When they restructured the CIB I was offered a transfer to the Stock Squad in Naracoorte. Dianne said there was no way she was going to go and live in the sticks. I declined the transfer and handed in my notice. She stayed in the force and moved out of the house.

I looked at Owen. "How the hell did you know about it? Were you bugging the boat?"

"Yeah. That was my job, mate. I had no idea you were going to be on it. I figured you must have just been a ring-in, but from the audio it was anybody's guess who was doing what. Anyway, the bottom line was five blokes went out and four came back. That was always going to be hard to explain away."

"Tell me about it."

"I didn't like what happened any more than you did. That's why I got out too. Working freelance, well, you'd know too. If you think a job stinks, you don't take it."

"Sure." Had I had a peg on my nose when I took this job? "So what do I owe you?"

"Nothing. I found nothing. I still owe you. If there's anything else I can do, just let me know."

I grunted appreciatively and we shook hands.

I went back to the office. "The mambo made me do it." What the hell could that possibly mean? Was it possible that all Owen's high-tech gear had missed something? Or was I just barking up the wrong tree? I put *Voodoo Suite* on again and looked at the cover. There was this half-naked, exotic-looking girl standing under a tree, with an orange glow lighting up her face, like she was standing in front of a fire. But why was it called *Voodoo Suite*?

I fired up the computer and did a search on 'mambo'. The first link was to Wikipedia. I clicked on that, and two seconds later my jaw dropped as if some invisible umpire had bounced it in the centre square. But the square was waterlogged and my jaw didn't bounce. It just hung there while I gaped at the screen.

> *n. pl. mam·bos*
>
> *A dance of Latin American origin, resembling the rumba.*
>
> *The syncopated music for this dance in 4/4 time.*

A voodoo priestess.

Mambo is a Cuban musical form and dance style. The word mambo (conversation with the gods) is the name of a priestess in Haitian Voodoo, derived from the language of the African slaves who were imported into the Caribbean.

Wrong tree! Hell, I'd been trying to pluck a splinter out of my arse while the world wood-chopping championships were in full swing elsewhere. But where exactly, and who was wielding the axe? I had no idea, but I had a hunch that a lot of sawdust would be spilt before I found out.

The phone rang. It was Ken Wallis, football manager of the Galahs.

"Can you talk?"

"No! I'm speechless!"

"What? You pissed?"

"Not really. But I might be onto something."

"Yeah well, you'd better get your arse onto a chair so you don't fall down when I tell you this—and this is in strictest confidence mind you—Brad's failed a drug test!"

"Really? What for? Steroids?"

"Datura."

"What the hell is that?"

"I dunno, the club doctor said it's a, a halogen or something."

"You mean a hallucinogen?"

"Yeah, that's it. Like LSD or magic mushrooms, the quack reckons."

"Why would he want to take that?"

"Buggered if I know mate. Brad denies all knowledge. Says he never heard of Datura. Personally, I believe him, but we need to find out how it got into his system. Like I said, this is strictly hush-hush, because clubs aren't even supposed to do their own drug tests, only the AFL, so we'll be crucified if this gets out. Did you say you were getting somewhere with your enquiries?"

"Could be. Not sure if it ties in with the drugs, though. I need to talk to an old mate of mine in the Drug Squad and try to find out a bit more about it. I'll call you tomorrow morning."

So, would I ring my old mate in the Drug Squad and ask him about Datura? Sure I would. But first I would drop kick a big fat pearl somewhere over the rainbow, and then sit back and watch the swine fly after it. Or maybe just crank up the search engine again. That confirmed that Datura was a powerful hallucinogen, used not only recreationally by some people, but also by voodoo practitioners to turn people into zombies. First they give them a dose of Tetrodotoxin, whatever that is, then bury them alive for a while, then dig them up again and give them Datura. Child's play, really.

Mambo, voodoo, zombies, Datura, drop kicks and fishing: I could see how the first four fitted together, but I couldn't work out what or who connected them with the last two. If the mambo really was a voodoo priestess and not a dance craze, maybe I should focus on finding her. There couldn't be that many of them in Adelaide, and they wouldn't exactly blend in with the scenery.

Chapter Ten

I spent the rest of the afternoon scouring the net for priestesses but came up empty-handed. I would have to get off my arse and do some legwork, and just grin and bear the groin strain. I might as well get something to eat while I was at it, so I went to the Dessert Pea Vegetarian Café in a side street in the CBD. I walked in and sat down at a little wooden table in the corner. The candlelight lent an air of mystery to food that would otherwise have been merely weird and cast a warm flickering glow on the wall hangings, made of certified non-genetically-modified fabric woven on warped wooden looms by oppressed minority groups who would look longingly at the unglazed earthenware tip jar as though it was the horn of plenty. I studied the menu, hoping to find something more appetising than cactus salad.

"Are you ready to order?"

A young woman in an ochre caftan with an orange sequin between her eyes was standing next to me, smiling serenely.

"Maybe. Can you tell me what samphire is exactly?"

"It's a plant that grows near here, in mangrove swamps and places like that. Some people call it 'sea asparagus'. It's very good for the digestion."

"Sea asparagus, eh ? Could that also be known as 'poor man's asparagus'?"

"I don't know. I've never heard it called that."

"OK, I'll have the vegan burger with steamed samphire, thanks."

"No problemo."

I leafed through the *Mystic Times* while I waited. It was full of fascinating articles about New Age therapies and advertisements for meditation retreats, but there was no mention of voodoo. I looked around. There were a handful of other patrons, ageing hippies in cheesecloth shirts, and young ferals with more piercings than my old Meccano set, nibbling on bits of dried seaweed and sipping soy shakes. I felt like a fish out of water. Hell, I felt like a hammerhead shark at a cocktail party.

I ate my meal without incident and was brushing the gluten-free wholemeal crumbs off my shirt front when I spotted it: a little advertisement in the bottom left-hand corner of page twenty-three. "Mambo Clarisse can unlock the secrets of your soul. Harness the power of voodoo and face the future without fear!" There was a monochrome photo of a black woman with a scarf around her head and a mobile number.

I rang it the next morning after a breakfast of ham and cage eggs, fried in a sea of GM transfats. The call went to a voicemail message, with drums throbbing in the background and a woman intoning in an exotic accent, "Mambo Clarisse is in a deep trance now, communing with the spirits. When she returns to this world, she will return your call. Please leave a brief message with your name, number. and problem. She will help you if she can."

I had my brief message written down in front of me. I read it out in my most pathetic voice:

"Hi, my name's Bruce. My wife has left me. I am afraid she is under some kind of spell. I need help to break it and bring her back to me. Please help me." I left my number.

I sat back, had a cup of hyper-caffeinated coffee with full-cream milk and three spoons of white sugar, and pondered my next move. How could I find out if she had any connection with the case? What did I know about voodoo anyway? Basically what an unskilled sign writer could paint on the back of my skull with a very broad brush. Maybe I should try to find out a bit more in the meantime. Find out a bit more than I could glean from Wikipedia? I seemed to remember some bloke down the pub saying you couldn't trust everything you read on Wikipedia anyway. So, who did I know who would know something about voodoo? What branch of human knowledge was concerned with such stuff? That would be anthropology, or sociology, or mumbo-jumbology.

Julie had done her Ph.D. in anthropology. Football team as diatribe or something. She might know something about voodoo. She could hardly know less than I did. I ought to ring her and tell her about Lucas anyway. So I did.

"Hello."

"Hi Julie, it's Bruce, Bruce Bilger. Just ringing to tell you that I may have a lead on Lucas. I think he's been living in a tent in the South Parklands, but he's cleared out. I'll check again later and let you know if I find him."

"Really? Thanks, I'd appreciate that."

"Not a problem. By the way, Julie, do you know anything about voodoo?"

"Voodoo? Not a lot. I've read a few books on the subject, and seen a couple of docos. Why do you ask?"

"Because I'm beginning to suspect that's what's behind this whole drop kick business."

"Voodoo? You're kidding!"

"No, fair dinkum. This footballer, he said the mambo made him do a drop kick, and at first I thought he meant the dance, but apparently mambo also means a voodoo priestess, and now—this is just between you and me—he's tested positive to Datura."

"Datura! You know what the implications of that are?"

"I'm not sure. Is it possible someone's turned him into a zombie?"

"It could well be, but who'd be doing that in Adelaide?"

"That's what I'm trying to figure out. I'm trying to contact a voodoo priestess, or someone who says she's one, but I don't know where it will get me."

"Possibly into profound guano, Bruce. Be careful. Be especially careful what you drink, or you may wake up with the mother of all hangovers. Or not wake up at all."

"OK, I'll be careful. And I'll call you if I find out any more about Lucas. By the way, does a man with a bull terrier driving a purple Saab ring any bells for you?"

"No. That does absolutely nothing for me."

Chapter Eleven

I wasn't sure what that remark about drinking and hangovers meant. Did she take me for an alcoholic? I went to the bathroom and eyeballed myself in the mirror. The whites weren't exactly snow white, but you wouldn't call them bloodshot either. I figured I looked clean enough to go and talk to the team's doctor without being sent off to rehab.

I was on my way to Paradise Stadium when the phone rang. I pulled over and took the call.

"Bruce Bilger."

"Monsieur Bilger, this is Mambo Clarisse. I received your message. I felt your distress. I will try to help you. Can you to explain me something of your problem?"

"Well, it's like, my wife left me and I don't know who else

to turn to."

"And you suspect that she is under the spell of another?"

"I'm beginning to think so."

"She has left you for another man?"

"Um, another woman, actually."

"Oh! It is a powerful spell she is under, but we have on our side a magic still more powerful. I will work that she return to you."

"That would be great."

"You can come and see me tonight at nine o'clock?"

"Yep, can do. Where?"

"In my studio. Up the stairs at number sixty-six The Parade, Norwood. Wear white or pink, and bring a bottle of pink champagne."

"Does it have to be French?"

"Not necessarily, but the Iwa appreciates luxury, so get the best you can."

"Sorry, the who?"

"The Iwa—the spirit. I will explain everything tonight. You are lucky. Today is Thursday. That is auspicious. Goodbye, Monsieur Bruce, and tell no one of this."

"OK, mum's the word."

I put the phone in between the front seats and drove on. Ten minutes later I was in Ken's office. He was with a man in a green suit, who looked like a walking advertisement for the therapeutic properties of sherry.

"Bruce, this is Dr. Walsh. Dr. Walsh, Bruce Bilger."

Green suit stood up to shake my hand.

"Dr. Walsh, sorry to make you go through it all again, but can you explain Brad's test results briefly, in jargon-free language, as far as possible, for Bruce's benefit?"

"Certainly. As you are probably aware, Mr. Bilger, the AFL routinely tests players for various drugs, both performance-enhancing and recreational, and operates a 'three-strikes' policy, whereby clubs are not notified of the outcome unless and until a player tests positive three times. The clubs themselves are expressly forbidden to do their own tests. However, because of his somewhat—how should I put it—bizarre behaviour, the club requested that I conduct a battery of tests for a range of toxic substances. We got the results of these back from the lab this morning, and there is clear evidence of the presence of Datura in his bloodstream, which is very unusual and alarming. In case you don't know, Datura is a potent hallucinogen with long-lasting effects."

"Yeah, I've heard of it. Do you have any idea how Brad might have ingested it?"

"No. He denies having taken it."

"Let's assume he's telling the truth and that he didn't knowingly take the drug. Could it have been administered without his knowledge or against his will, and if so, how? Could someone have spiked his drink, for example?"

"It's possible, I suppose. I gather the drug can be taken in various ways. I'm not sure how strong a taste it has and how difficult that would be to disguise if someone slipped it into his drink."

"Did anything else show up in the test?"

"No controlled substances, if that's what you mean."

Ken looked worried. "Are you suggesting he might have taken something else besides this Datura muck, Bruce?"

"No, I'm not suggesting anything, Ken. Just checking." I decided not to bring up the voodoo angle—not until I had more than a hunch to go on. They might think I was off my rocker and decide to dispense with my services. "By the way, Ken, could I talk to Kane Jordan sometime? He and Brad are good mates, aren't they?"

"Kane? Sure. He'll be around somewhere—probably in the gym or in the pool."

"OK. Has Brad got a manager, or an agent, or something like that?"

"Oh yeah, they all have. They all have someone to negotiate for them and deal with the media and all that."

"What's his name—assuming it is a he?"

"It is. It's still a blokey world, AFL. His name's Treloar, Riley Treloar. Smooth talker. Don't know how long he'll stick with Brad if he gets any deeper into trouble."

"He in the phone book?"

"Yeah. Look up Six-Pointer Management in the Yellow Pages."

"Is he Kane's manager too?"

"Last I heard, he was."

"You don't seem to think much of him."

"He's as dodgy as an Antarctic passport if you ask me."

* * * *

Kane was in the pool, ploughing up and down lane six, when we found him. He had a languid but economical freestyle stroke that propelled his lanky frame through the blue water at a fair rate of knots. Ken shouted at him a few times and eventually managed to get his attention. He swam to the ladder in the corner of the pool, hauled himself out, threw a team towel around his broad shoulders, and ambled over. He was about the same height as Brad but leaner, with blond hair that was almost green at the tips, the legacy of a lot of laps of the pool.

Ken jerked his thumb at me.

"Kane, this is Bruce Bilger. He's helping us out in regards to Brad and his . . . issues."

"Oh, yeah." He stuck his wet hand out and smiled. He didn't strike me as gay.

"I'll leave you blokes to it. I've got a meeting to go to. Let me know if there's anything else I can do, Bruce, or if you turn up anything interesting."

Ken stomped off up the concrete steps while Kane and I sat down on a couple of plastic chairs.

"They tell me you and Brad are good mates."

"Yeah, you could say that."

"I mean, you go fishing together and stuff like that."

"Yeah. We hang out a bit. He's a good bloke, Brad."

"I'm sure he is, so I'm hoping we can clear this business up so he can get on with his life and his career. But in order to do that, I need to know the facts. Has Brad ever used any illegal substances, either recreational or performance-enhancing, as far as you know?"

"Nah, never. He likes his beer, that's all."

"Don't we all? And when you blokes go fishing, where do you go usually?"

"Up the coast."

"Samphire Coast?"

"Yeah, up round there."

"In a boat? On a jetty?"

"Depends. Sometimes we stay overnight at our manager's shack, if he's not using it."

"Riley Treloar's?"

"Yeah."

"Just you two blokes?"

"Usually. Sometimes some of our mates come along."

"What about two weeks ago? Did you and Kane go fishing then?"

"The weekend before last? Nah."

"Is Wally Grunt a mate of yours?"

"Who?"

"Wally Grunt. Football and fishing legend."

"Oh yeah, I think I met him once. Wouldn't call him a mate."

"What about Riley? He ever go fishing with you?"

"Couple of times. We went out on his boat once."

"Just you and Brad?"

"Nah, there was this rugby bloke there too."

"What rugby bloke?"

"Dunno. Don't remember his name. He was trying to persuade Brad to switch codes."

"Really? Is that kind of thing common?"

"Nah, not really. Anyway, Brad wasn't interested."

"Anyone ever make any other . . . unusual propositions to you or Brad?"

"Nah. Sorry, mate, I gotta get changed and get out on the turf, or I'll cop a fine for being late."

"OK. One more question. How do you get along with Mrs. Spammin?"

"Tamara? All right. Why, what have you heard?"

"Nothing. I just mean, for example, she doesn't get stroppy if you blokes go off fishing and leave her at home with Samson?"

"Nah, she's cool about it."

"OK, Kane, thanks for your help. If you think of anything that might help us to help Brad, give me a call."

I gave him my card. He smiled awkwardly and strode off to the change room. The card would probably be a fistful of pulp by the time he got there.

Chapter Twelve

I went home and started preparing for my appointment with the Mambo. I dug out the white suit I had last worn at my wedding and tried it on. I was turning blue in the face from holding my breath so I could squeeze into the trousers when the phone rang. I breathed out, feeling the waistband cut into my belly, and picked up the phone.

"Bruce Bilger."

A thin, reedy voice sprayed a stream of angry words in my ear.

"This is Riley Treloar, Mr so-called Bilger! I represent Brad Spammin, and I would like to make clear that my client has been the victim of a vicious smear campaign orchestrated by a dirt unit operating out of a grubby little cubby hole behind the grandstand at Alberton Oval, and I will not hesitate to take the strongest possible measures to uphold my client's good name, in no uncertain terms!"

"Sorry, mate, you've lost me there. Who do you think is behind it?"

"Don't come the raw prawn mate, you know exactly what I mean, and if you don't stop harassing my client, I'll have an AVO, that's an Apprehended Violence Order to you, taken out against you . . ."

His harangue was interrupted by a dog barking. He tried to shut it up.

"Sherrin, stop that! What's got into you?"

By the sound of it, it was a chunk of Riley's flesh that had somehow got into the dog's jaws, and he was using the phone as a blunt instrument to induce it to let go. The commotion subsided, and he resumed, sounding just a little chastened, "Er, where was I?"

"Somewhere way out in left field where I couldn't follow you, mate. Listen, why don't we sit down and talk this over, man to man? I'm just as concerned about Brad's welfare as you are."

"Are you now? All right, what about eleven o'clock tomorrow morning?"

"OK, where?"

"Neutral ground. You know Al Fresco's, in Rundle Street?"

"Sure. Inside or out?"

“It’ll have to be outside, on account of the dog.”

Chapter Thirteen

I couldn't quite do up the top button on the trousers, but the wide white leather belt I found at the bottom of the drawer would conceal that embarrassing detail. Some disco fashion accessories are a lot more functional than people think. I headed off for my rendezvous, stopping off at a bottle shop on Botanic Road, which had a very classy bottle of Moet & Chandon Brut Imperial Rosé on special for seventy bucks. That ought to make any spirit's evening.

I got to the end of the Parade half an hour early, drove around the block, and parked the car around the corner in Sydenham Road. I slipped out and did a quick recce.

On the ground floor there was a shop called the Enchanted Broccoli Forest, selling "Only certified organic fruit and vegetables, and organic groceries". Next to the shop window there was a door with Mambo Clarisse's business card on it, just below the button for the doorbell. I walked back to the corner, crossed the road, and watched the windows from there. There wasn't much to see, just dim yellow light filtering through the curtains. But from time to time the silhouette of someone with big hair appeared.

At five to nine I sauntered down and across the street and pushed the button. After about thirty seconds I heard muffled footsteps coming down the stairs. Then the door was pulled back. She stood there with a brass candlestick in her left hand: short, stocky, black, thirty-something, wearing a dress out of *Gone with the Wind*, and with braids sprouting like snakes out of her head. She peered suspiciously at me and my suit and said, in a smoked-camembert voice, "What is it that you want?"

I felt like some total dag trying to get into a really chic nightclub. I said, "Mambo Clarisse? I'm Bruce. I've brought a bottle of champagne." She held the candle close to the label and studied it. She nodded, then turned on her heel and stomped up the stairs. I followed.

The room was something like what I had expected: wooden statuettes and old furniture, and lots of candles smelling of something more bestial than beeswax. No voodoo dolls or crystal balls though. Against the wall at the other end of the room was a low table, covered with a pink satin cloth. There was a big brass goblet on it and a white ceramic vase with pink roses. She walked over to it and knelt. I did likewise.

"We will invoke the power of Lwa Maitresse Erzulie Freda to help you regain your wife."

"Sorry, Lwa who?"

"Erzulie Freda is the spirit whom we invoke to help one to find a lover, or to renew a love relationship. That is her image on the altar."

"Isn't that the Virgin Mary?"

"She is identified with the Catholic Mater Dolorosa, as you have guessed from the sword through her heart, but her origin is in Benin."

I nodded, but my ignorance was showing.

"In West Africa, where many of voodoo beliefs and deities originated."

"I see. So how do we invoke this Freda?"

"First you will please switch off your mobile phone. The lwa will not tolerate any interruptions."

I did as she asked.

"Now we will offer her the champagne. Open it and pour it into the goblet."

I did that. Meanwhile, she lit another candle. Then she picked up a remote control and squeezed it. Drums began to beat. She started to sing. Most of it sounded like total gibberish, but there was something about a fresh, cool, beautiful white woman who doesn't eat people anymore. I looked at the pink champagne frothing in the goblet and started to feel very thirsty.

"And now, Monsieur Bruce, you will tell Lwa Maitresse Erzulie Freda what it is that you desire, so that she may grant it."

"Right. Well, Maitresse Erzulie, my deepest wish is that my wife should return to me, so that we can live as a normal married couple again."

I looked at Clarisse for confirmation that this was the right sort of thing to say, but her eyes were closed. She was swaying to the music, and then she started singing again, as the drumming throbbed away in the background. At least she didn't ask me to dance to it. I definitely did not have the moves, any more than the lamppost outside the window did. Besides, I was just about splitting my pants just sitting there.

I looked around. There was a closed door in the wall opposite the windows. It was hard to make out much else in the feeble light, except a white round spiky thing that looked like a demon's head, sitting in a glazed cabinet. It had a mouth that was almost human. After a while the lips began to move, and I could hear a voice whispering to me in time to the music. I couldn't make out the words, but somehow I sensed it was singing of death, a deep, deep death beneath the floorboards, beneath the froth and the foam and the seaweed that surged back and forth in my brain.

"Monsieur Bruce, the service is now finished. Maitresse Erzulie gives you her blessing."

That was a human voice. She was on her feet, staring down at me with eyes that bored so deep into mine they could have scratched my back. The drumming had stopped. I shook myself like a dog that's been for a dip in the sea and blinked to make sure I was awake. I cleared my throat.

"What do I owe you?"

"Me, nothing. You owe everything to Maitresse Erzulie. I will accept fifty dollars on her behalf. Unless there is some other service which I can perform for you."

"I don't know. What else does Maitresse Erzulie do?"

"Many things. She is a very powerful lwa. For example, she protects against poisons."

"I see. And are any poisons used in voodoo?"

"It is late. You should go home and rest now, Monsieur Bruce."

I gave her a fifty and headed reluctantly for the door. I wanted to ask for a receipt, but somehow that didn't seem quite appropriate. It would be like asking your local friendly drug dealer for one. As I stepped out the door I turned to bid her goodnight. She smiled and handed me the precious slip of paper. Maybe she really did have psychic powers.

Chapter Fourteen

I drove home, drank a glass of scotch, and replayed the ritual in my mind. What had I learnt? Not a lot. I still had no idea whether it was Mambo Clarisse who had driven Brad to drop kicks.

I went to bed and dreamt another weird dream about fish. This time I was the fish, and someone was pulling me out of the water. I surfaced again and again, each time catching a glimpse of the angler. Its face was shrouded in seaweed, like some kind of sushi mummy.

I woke up feeling like my brain was a jellyfish left high and dry on a beach and burst by some brat with a stick. Drop kick. Fishing. Poison. Pink champagne. Poor man's asparagus. Sword through the heart. Benin. I chewed it all over as I watched the toaster glow. Then I gave up trying to join the crumbs and picked up the morning paper. There was an interesting story on page three about a dead dolphin washed up at West Beach with a puffer fish stuck in its throat. I choked on my toast when I saw the picture of a puffer fish. It was the ugliest bastard I had ever seen. Since about nine thirty the night before.

Riley was sitting at one of the fake marble tables on the footpath in front of the café. He was wearing mirrored sunglasses, a purple sports coat, and a white shirt, with a shoelace as a tie. He had receding ash-blond hair pulled back from the crown of his head into a ponytail, and a wispy rust-coloured goatee. Specks of chocolate powder from his cappuccino had settled on his moustache.

And then there was the dog: a shovel-headed bull terrier with a studded collar and a pink nose that nuzzled Riley's ankle with the kind of affection it would doubtless be willing to demonstrate further by ripping someone's face off if he gave it the nod. That would give him an edge in business negotiations, even on neutral territory. It was making me more than a little edgy.

Riley declined to shake hands. I went inside and got a coffee for myself. When I came out again I pulled up a plastic armchair and sat as far away from the dog's jaws as possible.

"So, Mr. Treloar, have you got any idea what has happened to Brad?"

"Brad's a good boy. You can't believe half the crap about him in the media!"

"I haven't read half of it. What exactly are they saying?"

"You know: about him taking Datura and all that!"

"Right. Well, of course I don't believe that for a minute either. By the way, how long has he been your client?"

"That information's commercial-in-confidence."

"Whatever. I can find out easily enough. What I'm wondering though is how long he's likely to remain your client, if I can't clear his name."

"What are you getting at?"

"I'm trying to get at the truth. I reckon Brad's a victim of foul play, and I want to know who's got to him and why. You don't want to help me find out?"

"Yeah no, of course I do, but I don't know nothing about any fowl's play. I told you, I reckon it's the Port Adelaide team mafia."

"What makes you think so?"

"Well, it stands to reason, doesn't it? They've got more to gain than anyone else. If the Galahs don't make the final eight, the Power probably will. If I were you, I'd follow up that line of enquiry very vigorously."

"Would you indeed? Do you know Wally Grunt?"

"Not intimately."

"Well, I'm relieved to hear that. Ever been fishing with him?"

He pulled a silver ball point pen out of his shirt pocket and fidgeted constantly with it, sniffing it like it was a panatella, then sticking it behind his ear for five seconds before shoving it in his mouth. Maybe he had just given up smoking. After a while I began to sense his eyes roving relentlessly behind his shades, as though in search of a lucky dollar hidden somewhere in the landscape.

"Yeah, I think I did once, with a bunch of blokes from the club. Few years ago now. What's he got to do with it?"

"Dunno, maybe nothing, but apparently he had this thing about bringing back the drop kick."

"The drop kick? Get real!"

"Yeah, it does sound a bit wacky, doesn't it? But then everything about this case sounds a bit weird. You like fishing then?"

"Don't mind a spot of fishing now and then. It's very relaxing, you know: out there on the water, with your mates, a couple of beers, not a care in the world."

"Yeah, nice. Where's your favourite fishing spot then?"

"Some good places up Spencer Gulf."

"Good snapper up there, they tell me."

"Yeah, I've caught some lovely snapper up there."

I nodded at the dog. "He like snapper?"

"What? Does he look like a cat? He likes to run around up there, though. Likes the wide-open spaces."

"Yeah, I bet. What about Lucas Stokes. Know him?"

"Never heard of him. What does he play?"

"I don't know. Chess, probably."

"Chess? I don't represent any chess players."

"You should look into it. There's big money in chess. People bet a lot on it too. And how would anyone ever know if a chess game had been fixed?"

I don't know what made me say that. I just had this mental image of him watching two cockroaches climbing up the wall, pumping one full of steroids and the other full of some date-rape drug, and then talking some punters into betting on the second one.

There was a little twitch at the corner of his mouth beneath his goatee. He held the pen like a dagger and stabbed a paper napkin with it. The dog growled, right on cue. I wrapped my hand around my empty coffee cup, wondering how big a dent it could make in the animal's skull.

"What are you insinuating, Mr. Bilger?"

"Nothing. Nothing at all. Thanks for your time, Mr. Treloar. You've been a big help," I said in my sincerest voice. I stood up and walked a couple of blocks to the Government Information Centre in Grenfell Street. I spent an hour or so in the office of the Land Services Group on Level Two, where I found out that one Riley Treloar owned a shack at Middle Beach, on the Samphire Coast. Then I went back to the tent village. The derro said Lucas hadn't shown up. I figured he was probably at the shack. It had to be worth a trip out there. I went home and got ready. I packed my Glock automatic, along with a thermos of coffee.

Chapter Fifteen

I set out about four o'clock, hoping to avoid the afternoon peak hour, but still managed to get stuck in slow traffic on Port Wakefield Road heading northwest out of Adelaide. It was almost six when I drove up Middle Beach Road and past the intersection with an anonymous dirt road. I stopped the car, took out the binoculars, and wound down the window. I could just make out another car parked on the track, half hidden behind a tree. I couldn't tell the make or colour. I did a U-turn, drove back, and turned into the dirt track. I parked a few metres behind the other car. It was a dark-coloured Saab. I had a swig of coffee, took the gun out of the glove box, and checked it. What were the odds that I would need to use it? They seemed pretty long, so I left it on the front seat. I put the torch in my coat pocket and the pepper spray in another pocket in case I needed to subdue Sherrin. Then I got out of the car and started walking down the track. The salty, swampy smell hung in the chilly air. There was no moon and only the odd star peeking through the clouds.

The clinker-built shack was quite big and stood on wooden stilts driven into the sand. The door was in the wall facing me, and there was a narrow deck in front, with half-a-dozen steps on the right going up to it. A light blazed through a cheerful floral curtain. There was a little white triangle in the bottom right-hand corner of the window next to the door, where the curtain was pulled back. There was no sound except the sea, the frogs, and the birds.

I walked across the beach to the shack and crouched on the sand in front of the open window. I could hear voices. I recognised one as Riley's.

"All right, mate, so last week we invested six K, and our return was eleven, right?"

"Correct."

"So, how about we put eight thou aside to reinvest and split the rest, fifty-fifty, as per usual?"

"All right. I've done a bit of fine-tuning to the system, feeding in two more data fields and performing some deeper regression analysis."

"That sounds very impressive, but I'm blowed if I know what it means. Can you break it down into layman's terms for this here layman?"

"It makes the predictions more robust, more reliable. Over a period of several weeks it will translate into greater returns."

"Hey! Now you speakee my lingo!"

I guessed that the man talking to Riley was Lucas, but I wanted to be sure. I crept over to the steps and got ready to climb up. Then the dog started barking. There was no point trying to run away, so I marched up the steps and was a stride away from the door when it opened and Riley stuck his carefully groomed chin out.

"Well, well, well! Mr. Bilger! What a pleasant surprise! You're just in time for the centre bounce!"

He stepped back inside and pointed ceremoniously at a wooden table near the wall opposite the door. Another man sat at one end of the table, with a laptop, a wine bottle, and two small glasses in front of him. He was greying at the temples, had an embryonic beard, and looked at me as though I was a distant asteroid of passing interest. There was a trophy fish on the wall above him. It wasn't a puffer fish.

"Bruce Bilger, Lucas Stokes," beamed Riley, and pointed to a wooden chair facing the fish. "Have a seat, Bruce. Sit, Sherrin!"

The dog obeyed reluctantly, as did I. Riley took another glass from a cabinet against the wall on my left, while Lucas picked up a remote control and switched on a TV fixed to a bracket on the opposite wall. Riley handed the glass to Lucas, who half-filled it with port and offered it to me. I'd been watching

Riley all the time, so I was sure it wasn't spiked.

Lucas muted the TV while the advertisements were on. Riley sat down across the table from me and grinned. He raised his glass and said, "Here's looking up your old address."

It was my first sip of port in a long time. It was mellow and woody. Would I be able to use it get these blokes to talk, or would I end up on the floor first? I decided to go in fast and blunt instead. I nodded towards the TV and said, "So who's your money on?"

Lucas looked at Riley. Riley shrugged.

"The Galahs, by a margin of twenty to thirty points," said Lucas.

"And you reckon you can predict the outcome that accurately, on the basis of some kind of scientific or mathematical analysis?"

"Yes, often enough to make it worthwhile anyway," Lucas replied calmly. Riley smirked.

"He's a clever bloke, this one. I never would have believed anyone could do it either, till I saw it for myself. And it's all perfectly legal!"

"So why all the secrecy?"

"Well, some people might want a piece of the action, which would make it less rewarding for us. And some would disapprove, especially the bookies!" Riley grinned.

I leaned forward and tried to make eye contact with Lucas. "And would your spouse be among those who disapprove of the way you are applying your formidable intellect?"

"Leave his spouse out of it!" Riley sounded almost protective.

The dog started barking again and ran to the door.

"Bloody hell! Can't a man watch the footy in peace?" moaned Riley and stood up. The door opened and Brad's wife walked in, wearing a pink suede jacket with the collar turned up.

"Tamara!" said Riley, spraying port at me.

"Excuse me for barging in, but you said I should come up and see you sometime."

"Did I? Of course, but . . . well, come in and have a seat. We were just watching the game. Is that all right? I mean, since Brad's not playing, maybe it's not much fun for you."

"No, that's fine. I'm interested to see what happens. Aren't you going to introduce me to your friends?"

"Of course! Tamara, this is Lucas, and this is Bruce. Lucas, grab a glass for Tamara, will you?"

"Nice to meet you both." She sat down next to me, smiled, and squeezed my hand as if it was an almost-empty toothpaste tube. Her eyes were even redder than the last time I had seen her. Lucas fetched a glass, filled it, and handed it to Tamara. He didn't seem to know her. Meanwhile, Riley sat down and started fiddling with his goatee.

Lucas turned the sound back on. Tamara drained her glass and turned to look at the TV. I feigned interest in the game and tried to figure out what she was doing there.

The Galahs scored a goal and there was a commercial break. Tamara swivelled to face Riley and asked, "So who's taking the kick-ins for the Galahs?"

"Erm, I'm not sure," said Riley. He had almost twisted his goatee into a piece of string. "I suppose a few players will be sharing that task."

"Yeah, but Kane will probably do the lion's share, won't he?"

"Well, he plays in the back lines, so he may well do a few, if the Lions score a lot of behinds."

"And Kane can do a lovely drop kick, can't he?"

Riley's voice went up at least an octave: "How would I know?"

I finally got where Tamara was coming from and threw in my ten cents' worth: "Because you've bet a bundle on him doing one!"

"What are you raving about?" His back was literally against the wall now.

"You didn't mention anything about spot bets!" said Lucas.

"Well, that's one bet you're not going to win, Riley," hissed Tamara. "And I want those photos!" She had lost me again. And she had found my gun, by the look of it. She was pointing it at Riley. "Come on, give them to me!"

"I don't know what photos you're talking about!" He looked imploringly at Sherrin for support. I hoped it was only moral.

"The ones you took of me and Kane pashing at the Galahs' Christmas party. You told him you'd show them to Brad if he didn't do a drop kick tonight. Kane rang me and warned me to get out of the house tonight in case you sent them to Brad."

"They're probably on his phone," I said.

"All right, give me your phone then. And the laptop!" Her hands and voice were shaking, but her resolve wasn't.

"But I need this laptop! It's got all my records and the formulae underpinning my project, years of work," protested Lucas.

"It's your laptop or your life, mate!" croaked Tamara, aiming the gun between his eyes. I could see that the safety was on, but Riley and Lucas didn't need to know that. She glanced at me and said, "I only kissed him because I wanted to find out if he was straight, you know?"

"Yeah, sure, I understand. Give her the laptop, Lucas. You'll get it back once we've made sure the photos aren't on it," I said in my most reassuring tone. He glared at her defiantly, then folded it and handed it over.

"By the way, where's Wally?" I enquired. "I'm surprised he isn't here to enjoy the spectacle with you guys."

"Oh, he's probably at the game. He likes to soak up the atmosphere of the match," replied Riley in an impressive simulation of insouciance.

"You mean he's not in on the fix?"

"No! I mean there is no fix. Tamara's taken my remarks completely out of context."

"So you weren't betting on Kane doing a drop kick? How much weren't you betting?"

Riley sputtered, "If Kane wants to do a drop kick, I can't stop him."

I turned to Tamara. "Did Kane say when this was supposed to happen? Maybe we can still stop it!" I pulled out my phone and rang Ken. I explained as concisely as possible what was going on, and why Tamara needed to talk to Kane next time he was off the field.

Ten minutes later she had Kane on the line and told him the score. Riley sank into the hard wooden chair like a chocolate Easter bunny on a barbecue. Lucas sat frowning with his arms folded, glaring alternately at Riley and Tamara.

"There's one other thing I'd like to know," I said to Riley. "Did you bet on Brad doing a drop kick too?"

"No comment."

"And if that put a dent in Brad's AFL career, you were going to trade him to a rugby club, yes?"

"Why not? Some of them'll pay top dollar for a beefhead, I mean a well-built bloke, who can run fast and do a good drop kick. He could still have a good career."

"He's going to have a new manager, that's for sure," said Tamara, standing up, "so you'd better just stay away from him, Riley! I'm going, Bruce. It's not healthy in here. Thanks for the loan of your gun."

"Don't mention it. You want to take this to the police?"

"Don't be stupid!" sneered Riley. "The Galahs will be desperate to keep this under wraps. The AFL will come down on them like a ton of bricks if they find out they've been doing their own drug testing. You want to get paid, you'd better keep your trap shut!"

He was right, of course. It was a stalemate.

Tamara left, clutching the laptop. I put the Glock in my pocket and looked at Lucas. "So who drugged Brad to get him to do a drop kick?"

"It wasn't me. I just explained the biomechanics of it to him to help him perfect his technique. I had no idea he was under the influence."

I turned to Riley and gave him my most piercing stare, honed by years of practice on juvenile delinquents.

"Don't look at me! I had nothing to do with it! Wally and Brad went out on the boat a couple of weeks ago, just the two of them, and when they came back, Brad was really spaced out. I thought Wally was joking when he said he'd turned Brad into a zombie, but then he had him doing drop kicks on the beach and it was obvious the poor bastard would do anything Wally said."

"But where did Wally get the Datura and Tetrodotoxin from?"

"From his so-called voodoo priestess," said Riley. "Well, she told him where to find them and what to do with them, anyway. The stupid old fart wants to marry her. I told him she's only stringing him along so she can get residency, and she'll dump him for someone younger or richer as soon as she gets it, if that love potion she's feeding him doesn't kill him first. But he won't listen to me. Maybe you'll have better luck. He won't realise how hollow your threats are."

In the end I agreed to try. Riley was a snake, but a very shrewd one. And however shabby his attempt at blackmail had been, it was less dangerous than Wally and Clarisse's methods. I didn't stick around for the end of the game, curious though I was to see if Lucas's predictions were correct.

Chapter Sixteen

I drove home, stopping at a servo on South Road to fill the tank and ring Julie. I told her where I had finally managed to track down Lucas, and what he had been up to.

"Sounds like quite an eventful evening! And how did Lucas seem to you?"

"A bit spaced out. Maybe he had some of that Datura. It seems he can still crunch his numbers but he's pretty dysfunctional socially. Would you want him back?"

"I don't know that I would. I'm not terribly interested in playing nursemaid to a zombie."

"I can't say I blame you. I just hope it doesn't all mean we're headed for some kind of zombie apocalypse."

"No, it probably just means that voodoo is the new

Tupperware."

It was close to midnight when I stumbled in the front door of my humble abode. The phone was ringing. I picked it up and mumbled, "Bruce Bilger".

"Bruce, it's Dianne. Did I wake you up?"

I was speechless for a moment. Could this be the mambo's doing? Was there actually something to this voodoo caper? Maybe I should visit her again before she took off and ask for my hair back, or a uteload of really sharp business cards, or a genie to paint my ceiling.

"Bruce? Are you there?"

"Yeah no, someone else rang my bell. How've you been?"

"Good. Look Bruce, I'll cut to the chase. I'm ready to give it another go. What do you say?"

"You mean—us?"

"Yes, of course I mean 'us'. What else would I mean?"

"I don't know. You might mean 'the new Tupperware' for all I know."

"Look, Bruce, I don't *do* Tupperware any more. I've moved on. I've grown as a person. I swing both ways and that's just part of who I am. You'll have to be able to accept that if our relationship is ever going to work."

"All right. Actually, Dianne, I don't give a stuff which way you swing, as long as you don't spike my drink with Datura, or Tetrodotoxin, or any other voodoo-related poisons."

"What are you raving about? Have you been hitting the

bottle again, Bruce?"

"No, but don't put ideas into my head. Can we talk about this in the morning? I've had a long hard day and I need to lie down."

I hung up, swallowed a couple of Paracetamol tablets, and went to bed with a glass of scotch. I turned on the radio and tuned it to the nostalgic hits request show. I wasn't in a fit state to make major decisions, like whether to trade my boring bland bachelor's existence for a swinging spiced-up modern open relationship, for which I might well need some of the mambo's love potion. I drifted off to sleep listening to Carol Bayer Sager singing,

Don't wish too hard for what you want
Or then you might get it . . .

~

About the Author

Peter Tonkin grew up in Adelaide and hung out in the arty fringe there, getting himself into bands, cabaret, films, theatre and other funny things.

He also played Aussie rules football for a team he would prefer to remain nameless—to protect the guilty. And he wants to assure his readers that during his time as a player he did not attempt to execute any drops kicks, although some of his more adventurous team mates did.

Peter now lives in Sydney and makes a living from his obsession with words as an English teacher, having followed a circuitous career path that took him to Tokyo, Cambridge, Barcelona and Prague before returning to these fatal shores.

He is horrified to have his book *Football Mambo* set out in

American, not Australian, style, but his publisher did it anyway.

Football Mambo is a humorous noir mystery and his first published book, though back in Adelaide he was famous for writing dramatic monologues and other pieces for performance, including *The Ultraviolet Catastrophe,* which he performed as part of an ensemble at the Adelaide Cabaret Festival. He also co-wrote and sang such infamous songs as *Drakes' Blood, Tiberius* and *Neptune's Wild Sea* with the legendary Purple Caesars band, clad sometimes in a toga and at others in makeshift Centurion's garb.

Peter was a member of the Mad Love theatre collective and appeared in its inaugural production, *Rancho,* and created experimental films, presented at the multimedia show *Within the Palm-Pressed Planet* at the Adelaide Fringe Festival.

Anyone possessing photographic or video evidence of any of the above and expecting to profit from it would be well advised to encourage their families and friends to buy copies of *Football Mambo* on the basis of rational self-interest.

Find Peter at www.cyberworldpublishing.com and http://glomoid.wordpress.com/.

Our authors appreciate it when readers leave reviews of their work at distributor and review sites.

Cyberworld Publishing

All books available in e-book: an * denotes books are also available in paperback.

Books by Robin Hillard

Archie's Antiques Mystery Puzzles Book 1 (E-book only
Archie's Antiques Mystery Puzzles Book 2 (E-book only
Archie's Antiques Mystery Puzzles Books 1 & 2 (Paperback only)*
Ridgeway Murder*

Books by Peter Tonkin

Football Mambo*

Books by Olivia Stowe

Mystery Romance

Restoring the Castle*

The Charlotte Diamond mystery series

By The Howling (Book 1)*
Retired with Prejudice (Book 2)*
Coast to Coast (Book 3)*
An Inconvenient Death (Book 4)*
What's The Point? (Book 5)*
White Orchid Found (Book 6)*
Curtain Call (Book 7)*
Horrid Honeymoon (Book 8)*
Making Room at Christmas (Seasonal Special)
Cassandra's last Spotlight (Seasonal Special)
Charlotte Diamond Mysteries Bundle 1 (Books 1&2)
Charlotte Diamond Mysteries Bundle 2 (Books 3&4)
Charlotte Diamond Mysteries Bundle 3 (Books 5&6)

The Savannah Series

Chatham Square*
Savannah Time*

Olivia's Inspirational Christmas collections

Christmas Seconds (2011)*

Spirit of Christmas (2010)*

Books by Stephen Bush

No Regrets

My Sister's Funeral: A Murder mystery*

Books by Gina Drew

The Koniotis Mysteries Series: each book in this six part Cyprus set series, which travels from the islands past to its future, stands alone, but they are also all connected in various ways and form the different parts of one story.

Laughter's Echo*

Salted Away*

Mouflon Brigade*

Amathus Armageddon*

Bogus Bills*

Homewrecker*

~

www.ingramcontent.com/pod-product-compliance
Lightning Source LLC
LaVergne TN
LVHW050935080826
845145LV00004B/1269

* 9 7 8 1 9 2 2 1 8 7 7 1 0 *